Sweetbrier Sett

A Milkweed Christmas

Sweetbrier Sett
A Milkweed Christmas

Written and illustrated by

Kaaren Poole

Front cover and all illustrations by Kaaren Poole

Book design by Kaaren Poole

ISBN: 978-1-7375380-0-4

First printing edition 2021

Kaaren Poole
5280 Old French Town Road
Shingle Springs, CA 95682

www.kaarenpoole.com

Preface

Welcome to this, the second book in my Milkweed Manor Christmas book series. In the first book, *A Milkweed Christmas, The Inn at Ivy Knoll*, the hares of the inn hosted the centerpiece of the holiday season, the Christmas Day celebration. Now it's the badgers' turn. They'll make the season magical with a special performance at their sett.

As always, Milkweed celebrates the entire Christmas season, not just the day itself. So, here you'll share in the many activities happening around the community. Also, the animals are pleased to share a few of their favorite holiday recipes. They and I hope you enjoy *A Milkweed Christmas at Sweetbrier Sett*, and that it will be part of your holiday tradition for years to come.

The animals you will meet here are the characters from my Milkweed Manor series. If you enjoy these Christmas books, I think you will enjoy those too. You can find out all about them on my website, www.KaarenPoole.com or by searching Amazon.com or Lulu.com with Kaaren Poole as author.

DEDICATED WITH LOVE
TO ALL MY WILD NEIGHBORS
WHO MAKE MY DAYS
SO PRECIOUS

Table of Contents

How the Badgers Became This Year's Christmas Hosts

Aspiring to become a diarist, Audrey, who could neither read nor write, for the time being simply spoke her diary entries to herself. Acquiring literacy was one of her goals but it would probably be a distant one, as it was mid-October now and an important question was on her mind. The answer to that question might well keep her busy for the next few months.

"Dear Diary,

"As Christmas approaches once again, the sadness of the season has returned. For the sake of my daughter and nephews, I will behave as I have for too many years now: carrying on with the season's duties behind a cheerful face, while internally struggling to push away the unbearably painful memories that press on me—memories of the brutal attack on my childhood sett. Yes, this has been my way of coping. But lately, I've allowed a tiny voice to ask if I must live the rest of my life this way—if there isn't another way, and if there is, do I have the courage to seek it?

"Oh, how I would love to say yes. But I don't know that I can because I don't think this is a change I'm capable of making on my own. If I could, wouldn't I have already done so? So, now the problem doubles. Not only must I find the courage to change, but I must also find the courage to trust someone else. If I try and fail, I doubt I could ever try again.

"I would be taking a huge chance, but it's a chance at reclaiming my very life. Colwyn seems the best choice for a confidant. I'll speak with him as soon as I can."

*****

A few mornings later, Colwyn and Audrey were sitting on the bank behind Sweetbrier Sett admiring the view, when she nervously spoke the entrée she had so carefully practiced.

"Colwyn, do you remember the day we met? It was here at the sett. You were newly arrived in Milkweed and were meeting the residents. We had a conversation on this very spot in which you revealed your fears about the future. And in response I shared the most painful event of my past."

"I do indeed remember. In fact, your words were pivotal in my maturing from a lost youngster to what I hope I am today—a rat who is a valued member of his community. And, you know, your compassion for a young rat you didn't even know touched me deeply and gave me an example to aspire to."

"Well, thank you, Colwyn." Audrey was touched. "I'm glad I was able to help. And you have indeed become not only valued, but also deeply loved in this community. I've always been grateful you're part of Milkweed."

"But why are you asking?" Colwyn was truly puzzled.

"I'm hoping you can help with something that's troubling me."

"Well, I will certainly try my very best."

"That terrible day at the sett has never left me, and its presence is preventing me from being truly happy." She hesitated for a moment, but Colwyn remained silent, encouraging her, in his way, to continue. "The holidays should be filled with wonderful memories. And I know there *are* wonderful memories of my childhood locked away inside me. But ever since that day they've been beyond my reach. I'm too afraid of the terrors that will flood in with them and overwhelm me."

"Being kept from the good memories of your youth is, indeed, a terrible thing. I know for me it was a long time before I could think of my youth without being sad and missing my family. But the memories would come frequently, bidden or not, and eventually the sadness faded."

"How I'd love to be in that same place, Colwyn, but I don't know how to get there."

After a lengthy and sometimes tear-filled discussion, they devised a plan. Audrey would host this year's Milkweed Christmas celebration, and part of that process would be to reclaim and share her happy childhood memories. She was nervous, but knew she had her friend's support. She could do it!

Word of Audrey's desire to host the holiday festivities spread quickly through the community, and everyone—especially Audrey's daughter, Gwen, and her twin nephews, Arthur and Percival—was thrilled!

I hope and pray this will be the new beginning I need.

The Squirrel Girls Make Advent Chains

It was the last day of November when Emma called her girls, Effie and Lily, into the kitchen for a special project. She had already assembled the supplies—coloured papers, glue, crayons, a ruler, a pencil, and scissors.

"What's all this, Mama?" Effie asked, her eyes shining with anticipation.

Lily immediately began fingering the pretty papers. She was ready for the project, whatever it might be.

"Well, girls, how many days are there till Christmas? Do you know?"

"Thirty-seventy," Lily ventured.

"No, silly! Twenty-five!" Effie was very sure of herself.

"And how long is that, dears?"

Lily knew the answer. "A very long time!"

"Indeed! And tomorrow it will be 24, and the day after that it will be 23. But wouldn't it be fun to have a way to keep track of the days till Christmas? It'll be fun to make, and then fun to use every day as we get closer and closer to the big day!" Emma remembered this very project from her childhood and today she felt every bit as excited as her youngsters. "Put on your aprons, girls. This could get messy!"

"Yay! I like messy projects best!" Lily squealed as her older sister tied the little one's apron strings behind her back. Effie quickly put on her own apron and sat down, ready for instructions.

The first step, Mama explained, was to use the crayons to decorate the papers. Effie wanted to know what she should draw, but mama said to just make pretty, colourful designs. Effie was very serious about her work. She pursed her lips and stuck out her little tongue as she made careful marks on the paper. Lily scribbled bright colours on hers and didn't stop until it was completely covered. Mama said they'd need four pieces of paper, so each of the girls began another one.

"Aren't mine beautiful?" Lily asked. But it was a rhetorical question, as she just knew, deep in her heart, they were the prettiest papers ever. Effie was finished with her papers too, so it was time for the next step.

As the girls worked, Emma gathered the finished papers and used the ruler and pencil to draw parallel lines across them. She gave the lined papers back to the girls and handed each a pair of scissors.

"Now just cut along the lines and you'll make pretty strips of paper from your pretty sheets of paper!" While the girls cut, Emma drew lines on the other papers. Soon, they had a pile of colourful strips. Effie's were all mixed up with Lily's, and the effect was festive indeed.

"Glue time!" Emma announced. She took a strip of paper, dabbed glue on one end, and pressed the end without glue over the glue on the other end. "You need to press the joint with your paws for a little bit till the glue sticks. Now I have a ring!" She took another strip of paper and followed the same procedure except this time, before she glued the ends together, she slipped the paper through the first ring.

"Ooo! The rings are hooked together!" Lily cried.

"You're making a chain!" Effie observed.

"Exactly right! Each of you make a chain with 25 links, then we'll see what we have."

The girls were quiet at first, concentrating on their task. But after a few links, they were comfortable with the procedure and continued, growing their chains link by link.

At one point, Emma noticed something special Lily had just done. "Girls, look at the way Lily made her last ring," and she took a strip to demonstrate. She dabbed the glue on one end, but before joining the ends together gave one end a single twist. When the glue stuck, she took a red crayon and put a big dot on the strip, then put a green dot on the other side of the strip from the red dot.

"Lily, put your finger on the red dot and run it along the strip—without lifting your finger—till you get to the green dot."

"But she can't!" Effie objected. The strip has two sides and if she never lifts her finger, she'll never get to the green dot on the other side. She'll just get back to the red dot!"

"Just watch. Go ahead, Lily!" It worked! Her finger travelled right along from the red dot to the green dot.

Effie laughed in amazement. "How did that happen?" Lily laughed too, but she didn't quite understand what was so special.

UE

"With that one twist before I glued the ends together, I made what's called a Mobius strip. Strange as it seems, it has only one side!"

From then on, Effie made her chain from the special strips instead of regular links. Lily's links went back and forth between regular and special with no particular pattern.

When the girls thought their chains were finished, they checked carefully to ensure each one had exactly 25 links. As it turned out, Lily had to add three more. Each girl selected two lengths of ribbon and tied a bow through links near each end of her strip.

Emma led the girls to the fireplace. "The fireplace is so pretty with the pine and holly garlands draped over the mantel. But it will be even prettier with your beautiful paper chains." She looped the bows through hooks in the wall, hanging the chains on either side of the fireplace.

"These are Advent chains, and they're a special way of keeping track of how many days it is till Christmas. Starting tonight, just before bed, take a link off the bottom of your chain. Each link stands for a day until Christmas. On Christmas Eve, there will be only one link left!"

"And then the next day will be Christmas!" Effie and Lily were fascinated with the chains and very pleased with themselves. That night, as they would do every other night until Christmas, each ceremoniously removed a ring from the bottom of her chain, then enjoyed a bedtime snack of cookies and hot chocolate. Over the days and weeks, the excitement built. Many times, they vowed to make Advent chains every year from now on!

Christmas Tea Biscotti

Audrey reveals that the secret to biscotti is baking them twice. For the first bake, form the dough into loaves. Then cut the loaves in slices and bake the individual slices to crisp them. By varying the flavorings and additives you can achieve a nearly endless variety of luscious teatime treats.

The ingredients:

5 c. all purpose flour
4 t. baking powder
½ t. baking soda
½ t. salt
½ c. (one stick) butter, softened
2 c. sugar
5 eggs
1 c. chopped pistachios
2 T orange extract
¼ c. grated orange rind

1. Preheat oven to 350°. Prepare two baking sheets by greasing them or lining them with parchment paper.
2. Thoroughly mix the flour, baking powder, baking soda, salt, and orange rind in a bowl or on a piece of waxed paper.
3. In a mixer, beat the butter and sugar until light and fluffy. Add the eggs one at a time, beating after each addition. Add the orange extract and beat again.
4. Add the dry ingredients to the wet ones, about a quarter at a time, mixing after each addition. Mix in the pistachios. The dough will be heavy and sticky.
5. Working on a floured surface, form the dough into six loaves approximately 4 inches wide and ¾ inches thick. Place the loaves on the prepared baking sheets and bake at 350° for 15 to 20 minutes, rotating the loaves halfway through the bake time.
6. Remove the loaves from the oven and let them cool 10 minutes. Slice them into ¾” thick slices. Place the slices cut side up and bake for 5 to 10 minutes until browned to your taste. Let them cool on a wire rack. When they’re cool, store them in an air-tight container.

Arthur and Percival Join in the Festive Spirit

Just like all the other youngsters in Milkweed, Arthur and Percival had truly enjoyed Christmas for as long as they could remember. But this year would be even more special—the badgers would be hosting the community's celebration at Sweetbrier Sett. Early in the autumn, Audrey had made the offer, and the community accepted immediately. Planning had begun that very day and was continuing still at the beginning of December.

Audrey was focused on decorating and food, whilst Gwen had the entertainment firmly in paw.

This morning found Arthur and Percival in their favorite spot, perched on two moss-covered rocks a little ways into the forest. They were contemplating what their own unique contribution could be. It had to be memorable and spectacular, something that would be truly their own, and maybe something whose usefulness wouldn't be limited to the Christmas season. But what? They were stumped! And time was flying by!

"Percy, lad, what if we think through how Christmas Eve and Christmas Day will go and maybe as we do, something we need but don't have will show itself!"

"Great idea, Arthur! I imagine the rats, Colwyn, Elayne, and Michele, along with little Itsy, coming along the path to the sett. Aunt Audrey would be watching for our guests, standing right there at the door to greet them and show them in."

"Yes. Now here come the squirrels. Same thing—greeting them at the door and inviting them in. Some of the animals might have scarves or wraps, and Audrey would collect them and give them to Gwen who would probably pile them neatly on her grass bed."

"Uh-oh," gasped Percy. "Here come the hares, all four of them. There's Audrey at the doorway, but how will everyone possibly fit inside?"

"You're right. I don't think they can! There's our first big problem, but what can we possibly do about it? I don't think we could enlarge the sett. Oh, dear..."

"Oh, dear..." Percy repeated. They both sat in silence for a while. Perhaps an answer would come. They were both thinking—and thinking hard—but no great ideas were coming. In fact, it was such a long silence Percy began to nod off. But before he quite could, Arthur had an inspiration.

"I agree we can't enlarge the sett. But, Percy, we're builders! Maybe there's something we could build!"

That was the breakthrough. Percy snapped back to consciousness, and the brothers began chatting excitedly. The ideas were flowing, and to memorialise them, Percy was using a stick to make rough diagrams in the dirt. Several ideas were considered only to be discarded, but finally a promising line of thought emerged. They decided to rest on it overnight then refine their plan the following day.

Aunt Audrey was a bit concerned about the boys at dinner. They seemed distant. But then, Gwen was chattering relentlessly about her plans for Christmas entertainment, so maybe, Audrey thought, the boys couldn't get a word in edgewise or, more likely, didn't think it was worth the effort.

*****

The next morning, the boys visited the Inn at Ivy Knoll to consult with Jonathan, one of the hares who lived there. He was an excellent builder and also their mentor, and the badgers thought it wise to run their plans by him. Jonathan had a few suggestions, and once they were incorporated into the plans, he pronounced the project "quite doable" and a "grand enterprise."

I'd offer to help, but I think they're perfectly capable of carrying this off, and what an achievement it will be for them, Jonathan thought. "Let me know if there's any way I can help you. You were certainly valued assistants on the renovations here at the inn. And I think your project will be smashing fun! Good luck!"

Feeling confident and excited, the boys began gathering their materials and storing them in the forest near their sett. They knew their project couldn't proceed in secret, so they determined to tell Aunt Audrey about it over dinner and, of course, get her permission. As usual, they were eagerly awaiting dinnertime, but today they had an extra reason!

As the badgers enjoyed their meal, Arthur seized on a rare lull in Gwen's chatter. "Aunt Audrey, Percy and I need to talk with you about something important. We really want to contribute to hosting this year's Christmas celebration here at the sett and have a project in mind. We'd like to get your permission but we also want it to be a surprise."

"Not a total surprise," Percy added "as you'll no doubt see what we're up to fairly early in the process."

"Well," Audrey said thoughtfully, "I'm not sure I can give you my permission for something whose nature I know nothing about."

"Hmmm," Arthur responded. "Yes, that's perfectly reasonable. How about if we assure you that it won't have any direct effect on the sett yet will be an asset. We think it will be useful throughout the year. But after Christmas, if you don't like it, we'll disassemble it and you'll never know it had been there."

Percy was nodding his approval as Arthur spoke. *He's really good at persuasion! I hope.*

Realising he had said enough but not too much, Arthur fell silent. He and Percy waited nervously for their aunt's permission.

For her part, Audrey was torn. The boys had given her their full share of headaches over the years but were much improved lately. And she was pleased at their enthusiasm and desire to participate in what would be a very important event for them all. In the end, it seemed not only unjustified, but also foolish, to deny them.

"Of course, boys. That's lovely. I thank you very much and can't wait to see what you're going to do!"

* * * * *

The very next morning, bright and early, Arthur and Percival were up, dressed, breakfasted, and in the forest gathering more materials. It seemed like a much longer task than it actually was, probably because they were eager to begin building. Their first job was to trim six thick straight branches for the uprights. Using sticks, string, and a technique Jonathan had taught them, they quickly laid out six points in a near-perfect hexagon, the locations for the uprights. In a flash they had the holes dug and the timbers in place. After a quick check to see they were properly laid out, they filled the holes around the uprights, tamping the dirt firmly in place to secure these important posts.

Next, they installed horizontals between the upper ends of the uprights to form the base of the roof. More horizontals, about a third of the way up the posts, formed railings around the edge of the structure. But they left one of the six sides—the one facing the sett's entrance—open.

The boys stepped back to admire their work just as Aunt Audrey came outside to join them. Smiling broadly, she placed loving paws on her nephews' shoulders. "It's inspired, boys! A pavilion is my guess. What a wonderful idea!"

"You're right! Or you could call it a gazebo, or, if it were summer, even a summer house!" Percy said. Then Arthur added "We thought we could use more entertainment space for the Christmas gathering."

Audrey's smile broadened even further. "Indeed, we could! I've been mulling that little problem over and over, but didn't come up with any solutions, so was ready to just make do. But this is perfect!"

Gwen had joined them. She had a question. "What if it rains? Won't we all get wet?"

Leave it to Gwen to point out a problem, Arthur thought with frustration. "It's more likely to snow than rain, and if it snows, the snow will simply perch on the roof! But even if it rains, it should be fine. We'll make the roof sound with tightly woven branches, including a layer of pine with closely packed needles."

"Well, I think it's perfect, and I can't wait to see it finished!" Audrey enthused.

*****

It was a mere two days later that Audrey did see it finished, and it was even more wonderful than she anticipated. Clearly, the boys were gifted craftsmen with a flair for design. The hexagonal structure was open on one side whilst the remaining five sides had a row of small posts below the railing, standing straight like tin soldiers. Decorative touches graced the eves, and the roof was, as promised, sound. It could be counted upon to keep those inside quite dry in either rain or snow. Additionally, pine and cedar boughs worked into the roof gave the whole pavilion the inviting aroma of the forest. But there was more.

A safe distance from the pavilion, but still close, the badgers had constructed a fire pit lined with stones. A fire would take the edge off the chilly air as well as afford another place for guests to gather. Audrey thought it was a stroke of genius and said so.

"Arthur, Percival, you've done a marvelous thing here. The pavilion and fire pit are the perfect addition to our home and will be an amazing setting for the Christmas festivities. I don't know how to thank you." Tears of happiness overflowing her beautiful deep brown eyes, she gave them a heartfelt hug and whispered in their ears "I love you."

Gwen said the pavilion was very nice, but needed decorations, to which the twins replied, "You're in charge!" Gwen took the challenge and began planning swags and garlands to make the scene even more beautiful than it already was. It was important to Gwen to add her mark!

Happy Christmas

Michele's Starry Night Onion and Mushroom Soup

This delicious soup is a holiday tradition with Michele. She brought it with her from France and introduced it to the Milkweed animals, all of whom savour this special treat. The star-shaped croutons add a touch of Christmas to this beloved dish.

½ lb assorted mushrooms, sliced
½ T butter
3 lbs. yellow onions, peeled and cut into ¼" slices
2 T butter
2 T canola oil
2 t. dried thyme
1 T flour
8 c. vegetable broth
olive oil
French bread cut into ¾" slices
Grated Gruyere cheese

1. Melt the ½ T butter in a skillet and saute the mushrooms till tender. Set aside.
2. In a large pan, melt the 2T butter with the canola oil. Stir in the onions. Stir frequently until they caramelize—that is, turn a rich brown.
3. Add the thyme and flour and stir for two minutes.
4. Add the broth and mushrooms and stir.
5. Using a cookie cutter, cut the bread into star shapes. If they're small, make two per serving, otherwise, just one.
6. Lightly brush one side of each bread star with olive oil and place on a cookie sheet lined with parchment paper. Bake at 350° for 4 minutes. Remove the sheet from the oven. Turn the stars over and brush the other side with olive oil. Return to the oven for 4 more minutes or until the stars are crisp.
7. Fill individual bowls with the soup. Float the bread stars on top and cover them generously with grated gruyere cheese. (Alternatively, if you have oven proof bowls, prepare the bowls as before, but pop them under a broiler to melt the cheese.

sugar
flour

Holiday Salted Caramel Trifle

In honour of this very special Christmas, Evie was determined to make a truly amazing dessert. She hopes you'll enjoy it every bit as much as her friends and family have.

There are several steps to creating this delight. Evie explains that if you like, you can make the cake and toast the pecans ahead of time. Then, the day you plan to serve the trifle, make the pudding, whip the cream, then use the prepared cake cubes and toasted pecans to assemble the dessert.

You'll want to serve the trifle in either individual glass bowls or a single large bowl the right size for your number of guests. But the following recipes for the components are "one size fits most." You may end up with extra cake, pudding, or whipped cream, but there are worse things!

First, make the orange cake.

Cubes of this delicately flavored cake are the basis of the trifle. Use a 9" tube pan. Bake the cake at 350° for 50 - 55 minutes, or until a toothpick inserted in the center comes out clean.

You'll need:

1 orange
7 eggs, separated
2 c. flour
1 ½ c. sugar
1 T baking powder
1 t salt
½ c, canola oil
1 t vanilla extract
1 t orange extract
½ t cream of tartar

1. Grease the tube pan then dust with flour. Preheat the oven to 350°.
2. Zest the orange for 1 T grated orange peel and set aside. Squeeze the orange then add enough water to the juice to make ¾ c liquid and set aside.
3. Combine the flour, sugar, baking powder, and salt in a large bowl.

4. Combine the 7 egg yolks, the juice/water mixture, the canola oil, the grated orange peel, the vanilla, and the orange extract. Mix well.
5. Add the wet ingredients to the dry ingredients and incorporate thoroughly.
6. In a clean mixer bowl, add the cream of tartar to the 7 egg whites and beat until the whites form stiff peaks.
7. Fold the beaten egg whites into the batter.
8. Pour the batter into the prepared loaf pan and bake 50 - 55 minutes or until a toothpick inserted in the center comes out clean.
9. Cool on a rack for 15 minutes, then turn the cake out onto the rack and cool completely.
10. Cut 1" slices of the cake, then cut the slices into 1" cubes. Cut enough for the cake cubes to take up about two-thirds the total volume of your trifle. Store them in the refrigerator until you're ready to assemble the dessert. If you have leftover cake, you can refrigerate or freeze it for later.

Next, Prepare the pecans:

¾ c. pecan halves or pieces

1. Spread the pecans in a single layer on a cookie sheet. Bake at 300° for 8 minutes. Cool then coarsely chop.

You can get this far ahead of time. On the day, or the day before you're going to serve the trifle, make and cool the pudding, make the whipped cream, and assemble the trifle as follows.

Make the salted caramel pudding:

First, prepare the caramel:

You'll need:

1 c. granulated sugar
½ c. heavy whipping cream at room temperature
¼ t. sea salt

2 T butter
½ t. vanilla extract

1. Heat the sugar in a saucepan over medium heat. Stir constantly until the sugar melts and turns a deep amber. Be sure to keep stirring to prevent burning, and as soon as it's deep amber, take it off the heat.
2. Allow the mixture to cool for a few minutes then add the whipping cream. Allow any boiling to settle, then whisk to combine.
3. Add the sea salt, butter, and vanilla and stir to combine. Pour into a pyrex bowl or large measuring cup and set aside to cool.

To complete the pudding:

You'll need:

5 egg yolks (you can freeze the whites for later use in, for instance, an angel food cake)
½ c. cornstarch
2 c. whole milk at room temperature
1 c. heavy whipping cream at room temperature
½ t. vanilla extract
2 T butter

1. Mix the egg yolks, cornstarch, and ¼ c. of the milk in a medium size bowl.
2. Heat the whipping cream and remaining milk in a saucepan until nearly boiling.
3. While constantly whisking the egg yolk mixture, add a small amount of the hot milk/cream. When thoroughly combined, add a bit more of the milk/cream mixture, again whisking constantly. Adding the hot milk/cream in this manner prevents the egg yolks from curdling. Continue adding the milk/cream mixture until it is all incorporated into the egg yolks.
4. Pour the mixture back into the saucepan and continue heating, whisking constantly, until it is pudding consistency. Take it off the heat and mix in the vanilla and butter, stirring thoroughly.
5. Add the salted caramel mixture and stir thoroughly.
6. Let the pudding cool.

Now for the Stabilized Whipped Cream:

You'll need:

1 t. unflavored gelatin
2 T water
1 c. whipping cream
1 T powdered sugar
1 t. vanilla extract

1. Chill your mixing bowl and beaters in your freezer for 5 to 10 minutes.
2. Add the 2 T water to a small microwave-proof bowl then sprinkle the gelatin over the top of the water. Let stand 5 minutes. Heat in microwave for 8 seconds, then set aside while you whip the cream.
3. Add the whipping cream and powdered sugar to the chilled bowl. Whip till soft peaks form. While still whipping, add the softened gelatin then the vanilla.
4. Continue whipping until stiff peaks form.

Assemble the Trifle:

You can assemble the trifle in a large serving bowl or in individual bowls. Using glass bowls allows your guests to fully appreciate your beautiful dessert.

1. Place a layer of cake cubes in the bottom of your serving bowl (or, alternatively, in your individual bowls).
2. Pour some pudding over the cake cubes, then add random dollops of whipped cream.
3. Sprinkle with toasted pecans.
4. Continue layering in this manner until your bowl is nearly full. Lay or pipe whipped cream over the top and sprinkle with more toasted pecans.
5. Serve with pride to your amazed guests.

DECEMBER
5
25 26

Pimento Cheese Bread

The bits of red pimento lend a festive touch to this tasty bread. This bread is delicious toasted but it makes great sandwiches, especially grilled cheese! Makes two loaves.

You will need:

½ c. cooked potato, mashed
¾ c. water from cooking the potato, warmed
1 ½ T yeast
1 c. milk
2 T butter, softened
2 T sugar
2 t salt
½ t coarse ground black pepper
½ c. cheese powder (available from King Arthur Flour or Nuts.com)
5 c. bread flour
4 oz jar chopped pimentos, drained

1. Have all ingredients at room temperature, except the ¾ c. water reserved from cooking the potatoes. It should still be warm—but not hot. Grease two bread pans, either 4" x 8" or 5" x 9".
2. In a large mixer bowl, dissolve the yeast and sugar in the warmed potato water. When it's dissolved, add the milk, butter, potato, sugar, salt, and pepper. Mix thoroughly.
3. Add 2 c of the flour and mix until the gluten begins to form.
4. Add the cheese powder and drained pimentos and mix again.
5. Mix in enough of the remaining flour to form a stiff dough. Knead until the dough is smooth and elastic. Turn the dough out of the bowl, grease the bowl, and return the dough to it. Set it in a warm place to rise about 30 min.
6. Punch dough down and turn it out on a lightly floured surface. Divide the dough in half and form each half into a loaf. Place in the greased loaf pans. Cut two pieces of waxed paper large enough to cover your loaves with about a 1 ½" margin all around. Grease one side of the waxed paper and cover the loaves, greased side down (this prevents the dough from sticking to the waxed paper as the dough rises). Let rise to the size of finished loaves. Remove the waxed paper.
7. Bake at 375º for 45 minutes or until nicely browned.

Remembering the Mice of the Forest

Sophie and Carmen, the Milkweed Wee Scouts Troop leaders, had conceived a special holiday project for the mice. The effort had begun a few days ago. In preparation for the project, the four scouts who were working on their 'naturalist' badges joined their leaders on a mission whose nature was to be kept strictly secret from the rest of the troop.

They divided into two groups, each equipped with cloth sacks. Sophie and two of the scouts went to the forest, whilst Carmen and the other two scouts went to the meadows. Both groups searched for mushrooms, berries, acorns, and other seeds—those items of nature's bounty which were especially tasty to mice. After a few hours, their bags full, they met back at Littleton Community Center where they stored the bags for the next day when the entire troop would gather.

At the appointed time, the troop filled the Center, and the mood was joyous. Garlands of evergreen tied here and there with bright red bows decorated the building. A festive centerpiece of holly branches studded with clusters of ripe red berries stood in the center of a table near the door, and on that same table lay a tempting array of Christmas biscuits and jugs of punch. Most of the scouts were already enjoying the treats and chatting happily in small groups.

None of them knew what the project would be but they all knew it would be fun. Sophie and Carmen were amazing troop leaders. They had the backing of all the Milkweed animals whenever they needed extra assistance. But this was not one of those times—along with their advisor, Itsy, they had everything well in paw.

Itsy tapped on her punch cup to signal the beginning of the meeting, and once the mice were comfortably seated at the worktables, Sophie introduced the project.

"We are all so fortunate to live here in Milkweed where we have many friends and community support. But not all mice are as fortunate as we. There are many mice families living in the forest and meadows nearby. Most, I think, get on quite well, but no doubt there are some who are struggling. And whatever their means, surely they'd all appreciate being remembered at this special time of year."

One of the little ones raised her paw, and Carmen recognized her. "Yes, Camille?"

"I've met a few of the mice in the meadow and they're so sweet. In the spring, we made daisy chains together. I like them very much!"

Carmen thanked her for her comments, then recognized Jack.

"And I've met some of the forest mice! They're really nice too."

The 'Naturalist' scouts retrieved the sacks they'd filled the previous day and set them in the center of the worktables. Itsy distributed smaller sacks as well as lengths of red and green ribbon. "We're going to make holiday gift sacks. Tomorrow we'll deliver them to the mice in the forest and meadows!"

Butch, one of the more ambitious scouts, had a question. "Will we get credit towards a badge? Maybe the Community Outreach one?"

"No, Butch. Not this time," Carmen answered as patiently as she could. "In keeping with the spirit of the holidays, we'll be doing this kind deed without expecting anything in return."

At that, all the mice children clapped, and a few cheered and whistled. *This will going to be quite a successful venture,* Sophie, Carmen, and Itsy thought to themselves.

It was easy enough for the scouts to fill their small sacks with selections of the luscious treats the 'Naturalists' had gathered. The little ones were careful to choose a tempting array for each sack. Carmen reminded them to put the firmer pieces, such as acorns or pine nuts on the bottom and the softer treats, such as mushrooms, on the top. Camille tucked a particularly colourful rose hip at the top of her sack. Her neighbors admired that touch and replicated it in their bags.

Judging by the shining eyes and wide smiles, everyone was enjoying their work.

Itsy passed out small paper tags shaped like stars and placed a few red crayons on each table. The tags were silver on one side and plain on the other. She showed the scouts to use a crayon to draw a heart on the plain side of the tag then color it in. One of the more playful scouts protested it wasn't Valentine's Day, but Itsy quickly reminded him that symbols of love are certainly appropriate any time of year. Finally, she demonstrated threading a piece of colourful ribbon through the hole in the tag, then tying the ribbon in a pretty bow to close the top of the sack.

At this point, a few of the younger mice needed help, and their neighbors were happy to oblige.

It wasn't long before the scouts had finished their bags. They were all beautiful. The mice were proud of their work and were congratulating themselves by finishing off the rest of the biscuits and punch. Their parents would be along shortly to pick them up.

But first, Carmen and Sophie explained the plan for distributing the holiday gift bags the following day. Itsy and Colwyn would help. Each leader or adult would accompany a group of scouts to a part of the forest or meadow to deliver their gifts. Colwyn had carefully created detailed maps for each of the groups, and those who knew how to read the signs of the sky and winds were predicting fine weather for the morrow.

*****

And so, the next day, over and over again, the same tender scene played out throughout the forest and meadows.

A knock on the door. A mouse mum answers, and the family gathers round her. When Mum opens the door, she sees a young mouse and an older one, or perhaps a rat, hanging back—probably the youngster's escort. The visitor is smiling and carrying a package, a fat, bulging sack tied at the top with a pretty holiday bow and a star-shaped silver tag.

The visitor smiles and, handing the bag to the lady of the nest says "Hello, mum. Happy Holidays and God bless you and your family! I'm a scout from the Milkweed Wee Scouts Troop and we all wish you and yours the best Christmas ever!"

A tear of joy wells in mum's eyes and the children chatter excitedly.

"Thank you, my dear. What a treat for all of us here. We will indeed have a Happy Christmas, and the same to you and yours. God bless you!"

Some of the scouts are more out-going than others, and those occasionally step forward for a hug which is always warmly given and received.

It happened that little Camille recognized her daisy-chain companions at a mouse nest she visited in the meadow, and Jack recognized his acquaintance at a forest nest. In all cases, both the givers and receivers were filled with love and joy, in other words, the spirit of Christmas.

Audrey's Favourite Christmas Memory

This Christmas, Audrey intended to make peace with memories from Christmas past. It would be the most important gift she could give herself and, indirectly, her little family. The violent destruction of her childhood sett had, until this year, formed a wall behind which her mind was unwilling to venture. But now she was ready to reach back and seek out the good times from her childhood Christmases. The bad memories would no longer be allowed to squeeze them out.

She'd gathered Gwen, Arthur, and Percival around her as she prepared to tell her favourite Christmas memory.

*****

"The sett I grew up in, dears, was a large one, with three extended families as well as our own. There was always something going on and lots of other youngsters to play with. Christmases were festive, busy, and loud! But the Christmas I remember most fondly was the one when my mum, dad, two brothers, and sister—who grew up to be your mum, boys—traveled to see grandmum and grandpa.

"The journey itself was long—two whole days—and tiring. But it was exciting to see new sights and places along the way. Our sett was in a large bank by a stream, but the land around it was open, with fields and meadows. We crossed them the first day, keeping as hidden as we could to avoid humans. Then, by the end of that day, we entered a forest which grew thicker and thicker as we travelled onwards.

"I remember that first night we took shelter under a fallen log. It was actually a few logs in a small pile, so there was plenty of room for all of us. It was beautiful, with a light snow falling. While the light held, we watched it piling on the tree branches and coating the forest floor. Once it was dark, although we could no longer see it, we were surprised we could hear it falling. I hadn't spent any really quiet time above ground in falling snow, and the sound was new to us—and quite surprising.

"The next morning, the rising sun woke us as its rays reached the fallen logs under which we sheltered. They reflected off the sparkling snow and created shadows of pale blue-violet. The birds were singing, their voices clear as silver bells in the crisp air. A light breeze was teasing snow off the branches in tiny tufts. It was a perfect winter day, and magical, being so close to Christmas.

"Late that morning we arrived at our grandparents' sett. They were watching for us and ran to us as we emerged from the edge of the forest. Grandmum's hug was so warm and tight, and I remember the smell of ginger on her thick fur.

OATS
TEA

"It was warm and cozy inside, with the scent of pine filling the chambers. From the array of treats laid out on the table, I knew Grandmum had been a very busy baker indeed. Among the treats, I noticed my favorite—gingerbread badgers!

"We were tired from our long trip, so we all spent the afternoon and evening in the sett, chatting, singing carols, laughing, and playing games. Grandmum especially liked a card game called 'Go Fish!' I'll always remember the giggling whenever one of us would challenge another to pick a card. "Go fish!" We children loved games, but I think Grandmum had even more fun that we did! Bedtime came too soon, but my siblings and I happily piled into one of the chambers and, after discussing the plans for sledding the next day, soon fell sound asleep.

"The next morning, I woke to the sound of laughter, and when I looked out the sett opening, saw my brothers, sister, Mum, Dad, and Granddad happily pelting each other with snowballs. They were all jokingly screaming whenever a snowball hit them—everyone, that is, but my sister Jillian who seemed genuinely offended when one of those chilly objects dared make contact with her!

"The smell of porridge soon distracted me, and I found myself heading towards the dining chamber. There was Grandmum, standing by the stove in her candy pink chenille robe.

"'You slept a bit late, darling! You must have been especially tired after your travels.'

"I opened my mouth to answer, but no sound came out! Well, there was a sound, but it wasn't the words I'd intended. It was an alarmingly raspy croak!

"'Audrey! What's wrong? Are you sick, sweetie?' Grandmum laid her soothing paw across my forehead and frowned. 'Yes, you have a fever! Come sit.' After settling me in a chair at the kitchen table, she bustled off. Returning quickly, she wrapped a warm throw around my shoulders and turned back to the stove. She lifted the teapot, poured me a cup of tea, then added a large spoonful of honey. 'Here, drink this,' she urged. 'It should soothe your throat. Mind though, it's hot!'

"As I slowly sipped the honeyed tea, I felt a tickling behind my eyes and before I knew it—and before I could manage to control it—tears welled in my eyes, slipped down my face, and I'm sorry to say, into my tea. Salty tea was the worst of my worries. I drank it anyway. I was miserable. Yes, my throat was sore, but worst of all was the prospect of spending a much-anticipated Christmas at Grandmum's being sick! *No! This just can't be happening.* But it was. And I was feeling worse by the minute.

“Just then, the rest of the family came inside, stopping at the threshold to stomp the snow from their feet. Mum and Dad saw me crying and rushed to my side. “We were worried when you didn’t come outside for the snowball fight, but I thought you were just tired from the trip and were sleeping in,” Mum cried in alarm. Grandmum calmly explained I had a fever and had lost my voice. All I could do was give Mum a pitiable look.

“You can imagine the distress everyone felt, topped only by my own. Jillian took my paw in hers and gave me a kiss on the cheek. Mum, Dad, and Granddad hugged me, and my brothers said, ‘Sorry you’re sick,’ quickly followed by ‘does this mean we can’t go sledding?’

“Grandmum put her paws on my brother’s shoulders. ‘I don’t see why. Missing out on your fun won’t make Audrey feel any better. Isn’t that right, dear?’ I nodded my head in misery. ‘You all go on about your day,’ Grandmum continued. ‘Have as much fun as you can. As for me, I can’t think of any way I’d rather spend the day than here with my sweet granddaughter, Audrey.’

“Grandmum settled me in her comfy overstuffed chair and pulled it close to the old-fashioned heater grate. ‘Here, put your feet on the grate. It will warm them, and you mustn’t catch a chill.’ She draped the throw over me and tucked it in around my sides. ‘I brought you a glass of Grandpa’s favourite ginger ale, and one for me too!’

“We sat in silence for a bit, sipping our drinks and gathering wool. I must have drifted off to sleep for a bit because the next thing I knew my empty glass was sitting on the table beside me, and Grandmum was reading a book.

“Seeing me stir, she put her book down. ’Are you feeling any better, dear?’

“’Rrrasp,’ I replied, nodding my head slightly to clarify the meaning my rasps and croaks weren’t conveying. I smiled at her, and she smiled back. I’ll always remember how sparkly and beautiful her deep brown eyes were—truly a comforting sight.

“’Would you like me to tell you a story?’

Once again, I nodded my head but this time more enthusiastically. She bustled off to fetch a cup of steaming honey tea, and as I took a sip of the soothing drink, she began her tale:

I want to tell you about a special time in my childhood, sweetheart, an event which would never have come about if I hadn’t been ill—as you are now. It was spring and I felt cheated that all my brothers

and sisters were out with the other young badgers from the sett having fun whilst I was stuck in bed. I could hear them laughing and shrieking, and sometimes I was so frustrated I actually cried.

My mum was tender and caring with me, and after a few days I began to feel a little better. Finally, one day was particularly warm for March, and Mum thought I could go outside for a bit. 'The fresh air will do you good,' she said. I remember how firmly she connected well-being to the proper amount of fresh air! Sometimes I thought she overdid it a bit—especially on the most frigid winter days or the most sweltering summer ones. But I digress.

Our sett was located on a bank not far from a river, and on the other side of the sett the high road to the town passed by. Everyone was playing noisily in the direction of the river, so Mum and I walked the other way—towards the road—and sat in the grass. We were enjoying watching the bees and butterflies flit among the wildflowers. Mum picked me a bunch of clover and I was weaving it into a crown when we both heard a clattering noise. It was coming from the direction of the road. We were curious, so we moved a little closer and sat down again.

The clattering grew louder and louder, and soon Mum saw a carriage approaching.

'Look,' she said. 'It's a carriage. And a very fancy one! I wonder whose it can be?'

Closer and closer it came, and we could soon make out details. Polished brass lanterns hung from the four corners of the coach. As the wheels turned, their shiny spokes reflected the sunbeams. Though the road was rough, the coach's suspension was so cleverly constructed that the cabin glided smoothly along. A handsome pair of dapple-grey horses pulled the coach. The driver was dressed in red, his coat trimmed in gold braid and fastened with brass buttons. He held the reins confidently and drove the team quite expertly. It was a glorious sight! But the best was yet to come.

As the coach drew by us, the passenger signaled the driver to slow. We could see a fine lady sitting tall in her seat. She was dressed in a lovely lilac gown and her glorious silver hair was elegantly twisted beneath a matching hat. A trio of curled plumes topped her chapeau, whilst hatpins tipped with large, faceted amethysts held it in place. Pearls and diamonds encircled her neck and dropped from her ears.

'I do believe it's the Queen,' Mum whispered breathlessly.

The Queen! I could hardly believe it! I bid my mind memorise every detail of this amazing tableau. The horses slowed, yet she passed quickly—too quickly. But before she did, her sky-blue eyes sought ours. I smiled with delight, and she smiled back. And waved! The Queen! The Queen smiled and waved at me!

"With that, Grandmum finished her story, but her eyes continued to sparkle as if with diamonds as she became more and more excited with the memory from her childhood.

"'I shall never forget it, Audrey!' she exclaimed. 'Never! I have been blessed with many marvelous experiences in my long life but seeing the Queen—and having her see me—is surely among the best. But now I will also remember this day, spent with you, as a very special one.'"

"'Me too, Grandmum!" I answered, my heart swelling with love. Soon my eyes drifted shut, and when I woke I remembered dreaming of seeing the Queen myself!"

Feliz
Navidad

Orange, Cranberry, and Walnut Biscuits

Bake at 375° for 10 to 12 minutes Makes about 4 dozen biscuits

Ingredients:

2 ¼ c. flour
1 t. baking soda
¾ t. salt
1 T grated orange peel
¾ c. sugar
¾ c. light brown sugar
1 c. (2 sticks) butter, softened
1 t. vanilla extract
1 t. orange extract (optional)
2 eggs at room temperature
¾ c. coarsely chopped walnuts
¾ c. coarsely chopped cranberries or craisins (If you are using craisins, soften them in warm water for 10 minutes before draining and chopping them.)

Make the Biscuits:

1. Preheat the oven to 375°. Prepare two cookie sheets by greasing them or lining them with parchment paper.
2. On a piece of waxed paper, mix the flour, baking soda, and salt.
3. In a mixer, beat the softened butter with the sugar and light brown sugar until creamy.
4. Add the eggs, orange peel, vanilla, and orange extract (if you're using it) to the butter mixture and beat till thoroughly combined.
5. Add half the flour mixture and mix till incorporated, then repeat with the rest of the flour mixture.
6. Mix the walnuts and cranberries or craisins) into the dough.
7. Drop the dough by spoonsful onto the cookie sheets with at least two inches between them. Bake two cookie sheets at a time, one on rack in the center of your oven and the other on a lower rack.
8. Bake at 375°. After 5 minutes, switch the cookie sheets from top to bottom rack and vice versa. Check the cookies at 10 minutes, but they may need a little longer to brown.
9. Cool on a rack. Enjoy!

Audrey's Diary, Christmas Eve

It was Christmas Eve, and the children were tucked safely in their beds, surrounded with the fragrance of fresh-cut pine boughs. Audrey sat at the entrance to the sett, looking up at the few bright stars not yet covered by the in-coming clouds. *Perhaps it will snow. That would be lovely for Christmas!* Still unable to read or write, Audrey spoke her diary entry. *Someday I'll have to learn.*

"Dear Diary,

Here I am on Christmas Eve, ready for tomorrow's festivities. A few months ago, I couldn't have imagined it, but I'll be hosting an open house for all of Milkweed. And rather than being filled with fear and dread of the memories it will bring, I am, at last, grateful to be coming to terms with my past and reconnecting–if only in memory–with loved ones lost so long ago."

She stopped for a moment, and thought of Colwyn, the dear friend who had helped her with the difficult decision to host Milkweed's Christmas.

"I've always thought I did a good job of making the holidays happy for the children even though, for me, they were filled with sadness. But this year they are clearly so much happier. Their faces shine with the excitement of having the community gather here at our home. Even their voices are different–more cheerful. And they've taken up every task involved in the preparation with such enthusiasm. Arthur and Percival have been utterly dedicated to getting the sett and environs positively ship-shape. Gwen's outdone herself in preparing musical entertainment. Everyone's done more than their share with both the baking and decorating. How often the sound of carols and laughter has rung through the sett. How fun it's all been.

"Mum, Dad, Jillian, Henry, William, and so many dear friends, how I've missed you all. And I miss you still. But I now know I've done you a dishonour by tucking my memories deep inside myself. It's far better to remember and celebrate what we had together. Surrounded with memories, I know you're with me still and always. Tomorrow's celebrations are for all of us here in Milkweed–and for you."

Just then a large fluffy snowflake ever so gently tickled her nose. Then another alit on her eyelash. She smiled as she blinked it away. The snow began to fall more regularly, though still lightly. Filled with the wonder of its beauty, she looked up into the falling flakes. It was growing dark, but the Christmas lights festooned around her doorway softly illuminated the scene. Still tilting her face upwards to greet the dancing ice crystals, she closed her eyes and felt them fall and melt on her face. It was a perfect moment.

"I am blessed and filled with gratitude." She sat for a few more minutes, enjoying the peace that surrounded her, drinking it all in and storing it in her heart. Then, when she was ready, she rose and went inside. She sank into her bed and closed her eyes, ready to dream of all those whom she loved.

The Christmas Performance

The afternoon was as perfect as Audrey could ever have wished for. All the guests had arrived gaily dressed for the holidays. Glenna was the standout, her Christmas-themed sweater dotted with her collection of sparkling Christmas tree brooches. But Colwyn ran a close second, sporting a long stocking cap striped with a rainbow of colour.

Though the air was crisp, the warmth from the fire pit Arthur and Percival had built kept everyone warm and their cheeks rosy. A smorgasbord of every imaginable kind of holiday baked treat stood against the back rail of the pavilion. The adults conversed in small groups, often telling special memories from past Christmases whilst the children alternately played games and devoured the treats.

As the afternoon drew on, Gwen became more and more excited. Curtain time for the Christmas program she had so carefully planned was only half an hour away. Her fellow cast members, Arthur, Percival, Effie, and Lily were costumed and ready. The stagehands were talking to each other, reviewing, for one last time, the order in which they would be taking props into and out of the performance area. They ensured everything was at hand and waiting in the proper order.

Over the past few weeks as Gwen had called rehearsal after rehearsal, the cast members had oocasionally thought she was over-doing it. Now, as they waited for the performance to begin, they saw it had all paid off. There wasn't a single case of butterfly tummy among them. They were confident and eager, even Mitzi who was initially reluctant to participate!

Aunt Audrey stepped to a spot next to the beautifully decorated entrance to the sett and, smiling broadly, brought the crowd to attention.

"Dear guests," she began, "I've so enjoyed our celebration together, as I hope you have..." At that point, vigorous applause interrupted her. She was pleased, but also suddenly self-conscious. She took a moment to gather herself then continued.

"I'm honored to present this season's very special Christmas entertainment. Please take a seat and, on behalf of the cast, enjoy the performance!"

Dramatis Personae

First Angel	*Gwen*
Second Angel	*Effie*
King Wenceslaus	*Arthur*
Page	*Lily*
Poor Man	*Percival*
Stagehands	*James, Mitzi*

As Audrey walked to her seat in the pavilion, everyone's attention turned to the bank behind the sett where two lovely angels appeared and then descended towards the crowd. As they reached their intended position near Sweetbrier's beautifully decorated entrance, one gracefully pointed to her right, to a spot at the top of the bank. As the audience looked in that direction, a character appeared, and then another, standing a few paces behind. The first was costumed as a king and the second, a page, both in dress from centuries past. Below them, another character stood. Pitiful rags hung from his shoulders, and he stooped under a bundle of sticks.

It was now dusk, and stars were peeking between gathering clouds. But soon the clouds closed ranks and it began to snow, the weather rebelliously ignoring Gwen's script which called for a clear, moonlit night! Fortunately, the stagehands had foreseen this possibility and had fashioned an artificial moon. Mitzi and James hastened to pull it part way up the tree behind the sett and tie it in place.

The first angel began to sing. Her voice was clear and pure, ringing through the chilly air. As she sang, the characters acted the lyrics. Some in the audience might have thought the casts' expressions, stances, and gestures somewhat overdone, but the majority of the guests thought they were just perfect!

Good King Wenceslaus looked out
On the feast of Stephen,
Where the snow lay round about,
Deep and crisp and even.
Brightly shone the moon that night
Though the frost was cruel,

When a poor man came in sight
Gathering winter fuel.

The first angel continued into the second verse. Then the second angel finished it, singing the page's words. As she sang, the page convincingly conveyed the location of the poor man's dwelling. During the weeks of rehearsal, it had taken her quite a while, as well as many trials and errors, to develop the perfect pantomime. Gwen was impressed and asserted "everyone will understand exactly where the poor man lives!"

'Hither, page, and stand by me
If thou knowst it telling.
Yonder peasant, who is he?
Where and what his dwelling?'
'Sire, he lives a good league's hence
Underneath the mountain,
Right beside the forest fence,
By St. Agnes' fountain.'

As the first angel began the opening lines of the next verse, the stagehands silently brought props—a basket, presumably filled with food and wine, and a small log. Ordinarily, stagehands moved and were costumed so as to attract as little attention as possible. But Gwen, desiring that all who participated in the performance feel special, had them wear matching hats, green for James and red for Mitzi, topped with impressive white pompoms which looked amazingly like snowballs.

'Bring me flesh and bring me wine,
Bring me pine logs hither.
Thou and I shall see him dine
When we bear them thither.'
Page and monarch forth they went,
Forth they went together
Through the rude wind's wild lament
And the bitter weather.

Although Gwen may not have welcomed the snowfall when the performance began, it was quite appropriate for the next verse which the angels sang in turn. First, the second angel, singing for the page; then the first angel giving voice to the good King's response.

'Sire, the night grows darker now,
And the winds blow stronger.
Fails my heart, I know not how.
I can go no longer.'
'Mark my footsteps, good my page,
Tread thou in them boldly.
Thou shall find the winter's rage
Freeze thy blood less coldly.'

As the angels began singing the final verse—the finale—the whole troop joined in, turning to face the audience. The guests couldn't help but stand and add their voices. The stirring music echoed round the sett's little corner of the forest. Everyone was delighted, but none more so than Gwen. The performance was a huge success, filling the spirits of all who were fortunate enough to be present that holiday evening to witness Good King Wenceslaus deliver his message of charity—a message all of the Milkweedians had long carried in their hearts.

In his master's steps he trod
Where the snow lay dinted.
Heat was in the very sod
Which the saint had printed.
Therefore, Christian men be sure,
Wealth or rank possessing,
Ye who now will bless the poor
Shall yourselves find blessing.

Truly, everyone felt blessed that day, blessed to be part of a community of such good souls. But, of them all, Audrey felt especially blessed. She had Christmas back.

NOEL

Epilogue

It was a few days after Christmas, and Audrey was tired. It seemed that all the preparations for and celebrations of the holiday season had drained every last ounce of her energy. But she knew spending time with her collection of rocks and minerals would rejuvenate her. Losing herself in every little detail of each and every piece was like warm milk for her soul.

Standing in the chamber which housed her collection, she took a jar down from one of the shelves and removed one of the 'fairy stars' from it. She knew they were fossilized sections from the stems of ancient plants called crinoids. But their common name fit their intriguing shape quite well. She paused a moment to reflect on the occurrence of the number 5 in nature. She thought 3, like the pristine white petals of a trillium, or 4, like the directions of the compass, or even 6, as in the number of insect limbs would be more likely. But here was 5, right in the palm of her paw. Then she contemplated the process of fossilization. What a wonder! She had many fossils in her collection. She even had a tiny insect caught in fossilized tree sap. But the fairy stars were her favourites.

She put the little star back in its jar, and the jar back on its shelf. As she reached for one of her best amethyst crystals, she felt a soothing warmth wash over her. Her collection was, as always, working its magic.

She noticed the shelves were a bit dusty, so reached for her feather duster and got to work. She found herself humming softly, but soon noticed the sound of voices. It was the children chattering happily in the twin's sleeping chamber.

"It was wonderful!" Gwen exclaimed. "In fact, it was the very best time of my life. I'll always remember how we hosted Christmas for Milkweed, and how our performance was the height of the season. It will be the memory of a lifetime!"

That brought a smile to Audrey's face!

Arthur and Percy thought Gwen was overstating it a bit, but they definitely agreed it had been a fine time.

"Yes, it was wonderful. And for me, the best part was building the pavilion. We'll be able to use it all year round and every time we're having fun there, I'll remember how Percy and I built it." Arthur was indeed proud of their handiwork.

"And *designed* it too," Percival interjected. To him, that was the part to be most proud of. He had always been the more retiring of the twins, and something of a follower in the shadow of his more assertive and self-assured brother, but now he was beginning to come into his own, surprisingly finding his talents in quiet, more intellectual pursuits.

This snippet of overheard conversation confirmed one of Audrey's hopes for taking the bold and uncomfortable step of hosting this year's Christmas celebration. The other hope was for herself, that she could begin to recover part of the loss perpetrated that nightmarish long-ago night when a band of humans who could only be described as the worst kind of criminals attacked her childhood sett. That cruel raid robbed her of so many family members and friends who met their deaths in the jaws of dogs or beneath the clubs of the humans. But in the aftermath, as a way of somehow coping with the horror, she denied herself of any recollections of the happy times before the attack. She simply couldn't bear the excruciating memories that would inevitably intrude on the good ones. At first, she'd consciously push away any of those happy memories. Soon, the happy memories no longer even tried.

This year had been different though. She took a big—no huge—no gargantuan step—and it had paid off. The children had formed treasured memories to last a lifetime. And she? She had poked a hole through a wall of pain. She could see her way through that hole to a full, meaningful, and joyful life. All she need do is chip away at the edges of that hole until she could fit her whole self through. And that's precisely what she would do.

"I gave myself the best gift ever: I'm reclaiming my heart!"

ACKNOWLEDGMENTS

I've been fortunate in all the support my family and friends have given me throughout this effort. I'd especially like to thank my sister, Michele, as she traveled this journey with me day by day. Most of those days were good, but a few, not so much. Whatever I was feeling–discouraged, not up to the task, fatigued with the seeming endlessness of the task, or dismayed by that all too common author's angst about finding an audience for my creation–she was there for me, and it meant everything.

My other sister Andrea, my daughter Audrey, her amazing family, my painting friends, my writing group, and my accountability partner, Judy, were all there for me as well. I don't think I could have finished this book without them.

A special thanks, also, to my daughter Audrey who contributed the biscotti recipe. One of the best parts of Christmas here is receiving the box of Audrey's wonderful biscotti. She's truly a biscotti baking expert.

*****

Just as I was nearing the end of my task, my dear dog, Fiona, passed away. I'm eternally grateful for the joy of being her person over the past twelve years. Aside from all the other wonderful ways in which she was in my life, she was my muse, and I am grateful.

Author's Note

Creating this book has been a labor of both love and discovery.

The world of Milkweed is such a positive place. That's not to say that everything that happens is good, or that everyone's feeling fine all the time. It's that all the animals really care about each other and do everything they can to make each other's lives better. And it's especially true at Christmas.

This is the second Milkweed Christmas book I've written. The idea for the first one came as I was finishing my first Milkweed Manor book, *Tales of Love and Courage at Milkweed Manor*. As I'm writing this, the second book, *Dark Days at Milkweed Manor*, is also published, and the third, *Hope Returns to Milkweed Manor* is written. I'll begin working on the illustrations as soon as this book is published, Hopefully, *Hope Returns* will be out around the end of the year.

Then what's next?

Well, I know there are other Christmas books coming. The hares hosted the first one, *A Milkweed Christmas, The Inn at Ivy Knoll*, and, clearly the rats, the squirrels, and perhaps the mice need their turns to host the holidays.

I've found imagining the stories, writing them, and illustrating them all magical in their own ways. It was late in life that I discovered I enjoy writing. I've always loved making art, especially drawing, and I now think of writing and illustrating books about these little animals as my own special kind of "mixed media."

Thank you for reading my book, and I sincerely hope it's been special for you. All the best in your own creative endeavors. Creativity is, indeed, food for the soul.

Kaaren

PS You can find me on the web at www.KaarenPoole.com and on Facebook at KaarenPooleArt. Feel free to contact me at kspoole@hughes.net

www.ingramcontent.com/pod-product-compliance
Lightning Source LLC
LaVergne TN
LVHW070218110826
845147LV00003B/600
9781737538004